PIPER GREEN and the FAIRY TREE: TOO MUCH GOOD LUCK

Book
2

PIPER GREEN
and the
FAIRY TREE

TOO MUCH GOOD LUCK

ELLEN POTTER *Illustrated by* QIN LENG

Alfred A. Knopf

New York

THIS IS A BORZOI BOOK PUBLISHED BY ALFRED A. KNOPF

Text copyright © 2015 by Ellen Potter
Jacket art and interior illustrations copyright © 2015 by Qin Leng

All rights reserved. Published in the United States by
Alfred A. Knopf, an imprint of Random House Children's Books,
a division of Penguin Random House LLC, New York.

Knopf, Borzoi Books, and the colophon are registered
trademarks of Penguin Random House LLC.

Visit us on the Web! randomhousekids.com

Educators and librarians, for a variety of teaching tools,
visit us at RHTeachersLibrarians.com

Library of Congress Cataloging-in-Publication Data
Potter, Ellen.
Too much good luck / Ellen Potter ; illustrated by Qin Leng. — First edition.
pages   cm. — (Piper Green and the fairy tree ; 2)
Summary: On an island off the coast of Maine,
where children ride lobster boats to school, Piper worries that
too much good luck can sometimes equal bad luck.
ISBN 978-0-553-49927-8 (trade) — ISBN 978-0-553-49928-5 (lib. bdg.) —
ISBN 978-0-553-49929-2 (ebook)
[1. Luck—Fiction. 2. Schools—Fiction. 3. Islands—Fiction.]
I. Leng, Qin, illustrator. II. Title.
PZ7.P8518To 2015
[Fic]—dc23
2015005271

The text of this book is set in 17-point Mrs Eaves.
The illustrations were created using ink and digital painting.

Printed in the United States of America
August 2015
10 9 8 7 6 5 4 3 2 1

First Edition

For Anne Mazer and Megan Shull,
because good friends are even harder to find
than a perfect strawberry.
—E.P.

For my sister Lian and our
secret good-luck code.
—Q.L.

Lighthouse

Piper's House

Fairy Tree

Ferry Landing

The Little Store

Peek-a-Boo ISLAND

Wharf

Woods

Double Cove

Peeka-Boo Island Harbor

Post Office

Library

Health Clinic

Fire Station

Tom Thumb Island

Goose Pond

Turtle Cove

Cubbyhole Cove

Blueberry Cove

Granite Quarry

Seal Ledge

Twin Sister Islands

CHAPTER ONE

THE IMPORTANT STUFF

My name is Piper Green and I live on Peek-a-Boo Island. When people hear that I live on an island, they think it's like Hawaii or something. It's not. There aren't any coconuts or hula-hula girls. Although one time I tied some garbage bags around my little brother Leo's waist and gave him a quarter to hula-dance in our front yard.

There are two things you should know about Peek-a-Boo Island:

1. All the kids on the island ride
   a lobster boat to school.

2. There is a Fairy Tree
   in my front yard.

Also, Leo is actually a pretty good hula
dancer.

That has nothing to do with this story.
I just felt like telling you.

CHAPTER TWO

THE PERFECT STRAWBERRY

I was in a great mood this morning. That was because today Mom was going to paint my bedroom lime green, which is my new favorite color.

"Remember to paint my dresser lime green, too, okay?" I told Mom at breakfast.

"I will."

"And the knobs on my dresser," I said. I scooped up Jibs and put him in my lap. He is my little gray kitten. His brother, Glunkey, was still sleeping on the couch. He's the lazy one.

"Dresser knobs, lime green. Got it," Mom said. She put a bowl of oatmeal down in front of me, and one in front of Leo.

"And paint my bookshelf lime green, too, please," I said.

"Don't you think that's a lot of lime green, Piper?" Mom asked.

"No, because lime green is the best color. It's the color of my cereal milk on Saint Patrick's Day."

"You know why cereal milk is green on Saint Patrick's Day?" Leo said. He leaned over and whispered in my ear, "Because it's leprechaun pee."

I ignored him.

Mom grabbed a bowl of strawberries

from the fridge. She took out a strawberry and began to cut it into my oatmeal.

"Not that one!" I screeched so loud that Jibs jumped off my lap. "That one's got a lump on it."

I am a fussbudget about my strawberries. And the problem with strawberries is that you can almost never find the perfect one. They're either too scrawny or they have dents in them or they have some weird bump growing on their skin.

Mom took out another strawberry.

"I don't like the looks of that one either," I told her.

"Piper, I'm growing gray hairs waiting for you to pick a strawberry."

"I think I see the gray hair," Leo said, squinting at Mom. "It's right on your chin."

Just then, I spied the perfect strawberry in the bowl. It was big and shiny and bright red.

"That one!" I pointed at it. "It's the most perfect one. I love it with all my heart!"

Mom sighed. She fished around in the bowl until she found the one I wanted. Then she held it over my oatmeal and started to cut it.

"NOOOO!"

"Jeezum crow, Piper, what now?" Mom said.

"It's too beautiful to eat," I told her.

I took the strawberry and held it to my chest.

"Well, what else are you going to do with it?" Mom asked.

"She could wear it as a hat," Leo suggested.

I thought for a moment. Then I had a brainchild. That's when a smart idea pops out of your brain.

I ate up my oatmeal extra fast. Then, while Leo was still finishing his, I slipped outside. I ran past the broken old skiff that Leo and I play shipwreck in, and then past the stacks of yellow lobster traps. I ran until I reached the Fairy Tree at the edge of our front lawn. It's a fat red maple tree

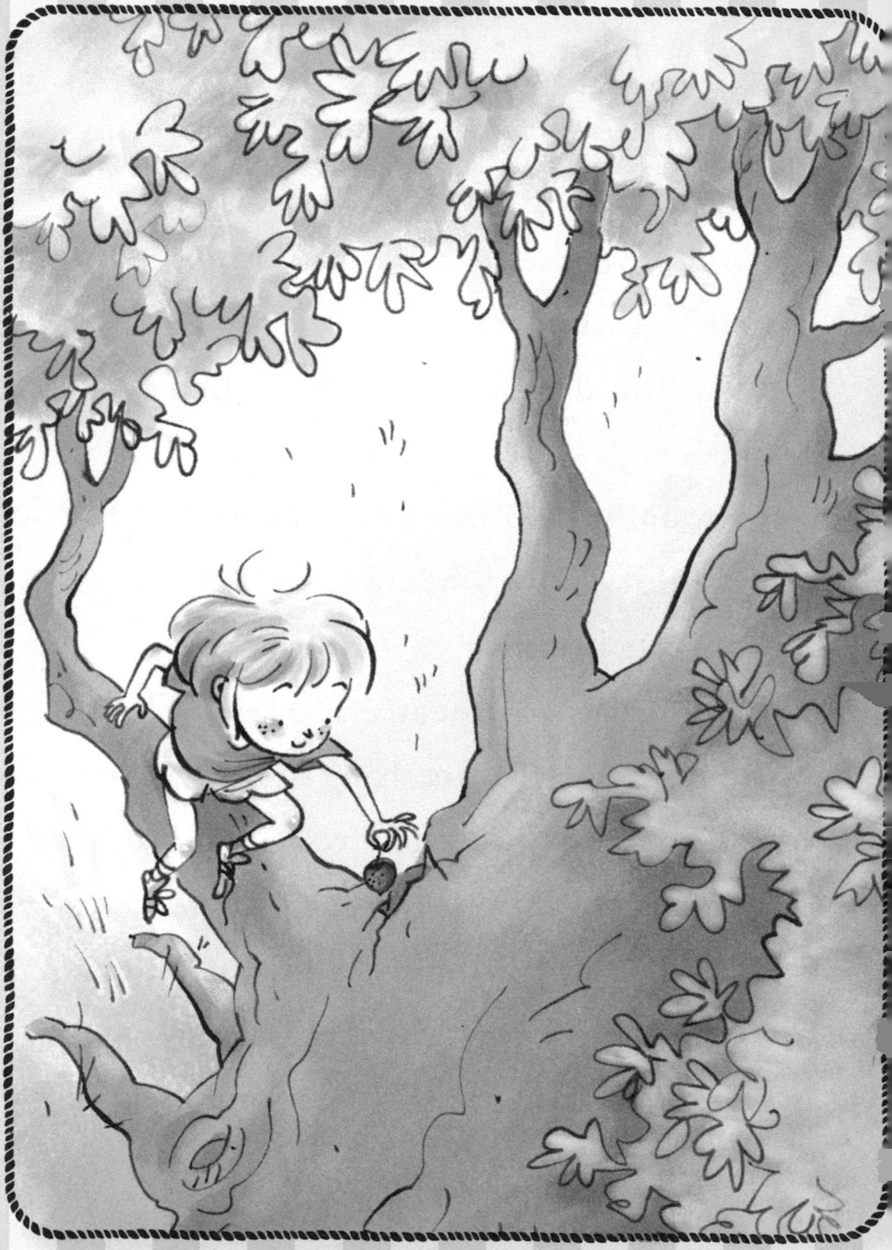

with branches that are good for climbing. I scooched up the tree until I reached the fairy hole in the tree trunk. If you put a treasure inside that hole, the fairies will take it, and in its place they will leave you a new treasure. The only other person who knows about the Fairy Tree is my neighbor Mrs. Pennypocket, and she is *very* confidential. That means she can keep her mouth shut.

I put the perfect strawberry in the fairy hole.

"I don't know if you fairies can hear me in there," I said, "but I hope you like the strawberry."

Then I patted the tree in a friendly way.

"And by the way," I said, "if you don't know what to leave for me, here's a hint: secret-agent night-vision goggles. No pressure, though."

CHAPTER
THREE

TOO MUCH GOOD LUCK

It was windy that morning on Peek-a-Boo Island. The *Maddie Rose,* which is the lobster boat that takes us to the Mink Island School each day, wobbled and rolled as we pulled out of the harbor. I had to stand with my feet wide apart so that I wouldn't fall down.

Jacob and I were the only two kids riding outside on the boat's deck. We always ride outside, even if the weather is crummy. All the other kids sit inside the wheelhouse with Mr. Grindle, who is our school-boat driver.

Jacob took a bite out of his cinnamon roll. Every day Mr. Grindle's wife makes a basket of treats for the kids on the school boat. Sometimes she makes powdered doughnuts or blueberry muffins or bear claws. But cinnamon rolls are my absolute favorite.

"Hey, guess what?" I said to Jacob.

He just looked at me. He didn't even say, "What?" He doesn't talk much. That's okay, though, because I am a motormouth.

"Today's my lucky day," I told him. I held up one finger. "Lucky Thing Number One: my mom is painting my bedroom lime green. Lime green is the best color. One day, when you get your own lobster boat, Jacob, you should paint it lime green."

"I already know what color I'm going to paint it," said Jacob. "It's going to be red and white."

"Okay, but paint it lime green. It's just a better color. Now for Lucky Thing Number Two: I found the perfect strawberry this morning. It was the fattest, reddest, most beautiful strawberry I have ever seen. And last of all, Lucky Thing Number Three"—I held up my cinnamon roll—"cinnamon rolls are my favorite treat."

I took a big bite. Then I made a face. There was something hard in my cinnamon roll.

"Hey!" I spit the chewed-up cinnamon roll into my hand.

Jacob looked at it.

"There's blood in it," he said.

"BLOOD?!" I looked down at the goop. It was true. There was a swirly pink spot on it.

Suddenly Jacob stuck his fingers right into the chewed-up blob.

"EWWW!!!" I screeched. "That is DIS-GUSTING!"

"Look." Jacob was holding something between his fingers. "It's a tooth."

"Mrs. Grindle baked a *tooth* into my cinnamon roll?" I said.

Jacob rolled his eyeballs. "Piper, this is *your* tooth."

I poked my tongue at my wiggly front

tooth. It wasn't there anymore. All I could feel were my smooth gums.

I smiled.

I took my tooth out of his hand and held it up. "Do you know what this is, Jacob?" I asked. "And don't say 'a tooth.'"

He shook his head.

"This is Lucky Thing Number *Four*!"

But for some reason, Jacob didn't look happy about that.

"Why are you making that depressing face?" I asked him.

"Because my dad told me that three lucky things in a row is good," he said. "But *four* lucky things?" Jacob made his eyes wide. "He says that four lucky things is TOO MUCH good luck. And too much good luck equals *bad* luck."

Jacob's dad is very superstitious. He won't bring a ham sandwich on his lobster boat because pigs can't swim. Also, he says you shouldn't whistle on a lobster boat or it will bring windy weather.

"Oh, *phoof*!" I flapped my hand at him. "I don't believe in all that superstitious stuff."

Just then, the boat started rolling even more. Jacob caught my arm when I stumbled.

"Careful," said Jacob. "If you drop your tooth, you won't be able to put it under your pillow."

I stuck the tooth in my pocket.

"Don't worry, I'm not losing this little beauty." I patted my pocket. "It's a front tooth. I get a whole dollar for a front tooth. *Ka-ching!*"

That's the sound money makes.

CHAPTER
FOUR

BINKIES

When I got to school, I looked all around the playground for my best friend, Ruby. She was playing cops and robbers with Nathan, one of the first graders. Ruby was the cop. Nathan was in jail, which meant he had to squat down under the little-kid slide.

"Ruby, Ruby! Guess what?" I ran right up to her and did a binky. A binky is this thing that Nacho does when he's happy. Nacho is our class bunny and he is the sweetest, most adorable bunny you have

ever seen in your life. When he does a binky, he pops right up in the air and kicks out his hind legs. Ruby and I started doing binkies, too, whenever we're happy. It makes you look like a total madman, but we don't care.

Ruby guessed right. "Is today the day your mom is going to paint your bedroom?"

"Yup! Lime green."

Nathan wrinkled up his nose. "Lime green? Why would you want to paint your room lime green? That's the color of the Wicked Witch's face in *The Wizard of Oz.*"

"Quiet, you!" Ruby said, pointing at him. "No talking in jail."

"I like your rings, Ruby," I said. Her fingers had lobster bands on them. Lobster bands are the fat rubber bands that they put on lobsters' claws to keep them from pinching.

"Dad gave me a bunch of them," Ruby said. She spread out her fingers for me and wiggled them. "Look, I wrote stuff on each one with a Sharpie."

One said "Superstar!" Another said "Sweeeeet!" And another said "I heart bacon."

"Hey! *I* heart bacon!" I said.

So she gave me that ring.

"Want to see me make steam come out of my nose?" said Nathan.

We sort of did. So Nathan puffed out his cheeks and made his eyes squinty. His face started getting all red. Nothing happened for a long time. Finally, some stuff did come out of his nose, but it wasn't steam.

The bell rang and we all sprinted upstairs to the classroom and sat down in our seats. Our teacher, Ms. Arabella, walked in. She was carrying her giant tote bag. She always carries that thing. It looks as if it could hold all kinds of interesting stuff, like stickers and binoculars and Bubble Wrap. But the only thing she ever pulls out of it is more work for us.

"I have some good news, class," she

said. "Once you all quiet down, I'll tell you what it is."

I thought about what that good news could be. Maybe Ms. Arabella was going to give us an award. But I couldn't think of anything that our class is best at, except for being "the loudest people in North America, for heaven's sakes." That's what Mrs. Woodlawn, the teacher down the hall, always says before she shuts our classroom door.

Then I remembered something. And suddenly I had an idea. . . .

"Ms. Arabella, I think I know what your good news is!" I said, jumping out of my chair.

"Sit down, Piper," said Ms. Arabella,

frowning. "And if you want to say some-thing, I need to see a hand in the air."

Ms. Arabella has long, wavy golden princess hair. She wears swishy princess dresses too. The only thing that is not like a princess is her attitude, which is a little on the crabby side.

I raised my hand.

"Yes, Piper?" said Ms. Arabella.

"The good news is you are going to have a baby, right? Because last week I saw you stuffing a hard-boiled egg in your mouth at lunch. And then you gobbled a second one. And after that, you gobbled a yogurt and a bag of pretzels and an orange. So I'm guessing you're eating for two."

The class got into a ruckus when they heard that.

A ruckus is when everyone starts yammering at the same time.

"What will you name the baby, Ms. Arabella?" asked Nicole.

"You should name it Matilda," said Allie O'Malley. "Only if it's a girl, though."

"Settle down!" Ms. Arabella said. "I am *not* having a baby."

"Well, if you do have a baby, don't feed it a lot of cheese," Garth said. "Because my cousin ate a lot of cheese, and he didn't go to the bathroom for six days. The doctor said he could have exploded."

"That's enough, Garth," Ms. Arabella said.

"Plus, you should paint the baby's room lime green, because it's the best color." I said this very quickly, before she could stop me.

Ms. Arabella shook her head at me and her face got pink. That's the color of her annoyed face.

All of a sudden, Ruby's hand started waving like crazy.

"This had better not be about a baby, Ruby," Ms. Arabella said.

"It's not," said Ruby in a worried voice. "It's about Nacho."

We all looked over at Nacho.

And guess what?

He wasn't there.

CHAPTER FIVE

BAD LUCK CAMILLA

"Someone stole Nacho!" Garth shouted.

We all got into another ruckus over this news. Ms. Arabella clapped her hands together.

"No one stole Nacho," Ms. Arabella said.

Allie O'Malley put her hand on her chest and gasped. "Oh no! Did he meet an untimely end?"

"What does that mean?" Nicole asked.

"She means, did Nacho *die*," said Ruby.

There was a brand-new ruckus over that

one. But Ms. Arabella said, "Now if you'd all simmer down, I'll explain about Nacho and tell you the good news."

We tried to simmer down.

"The good news is that we are going to have a new student in our class." Ms. Arabella smiled at us. "Her name is Camilla, and tomorrow will be her first day."

"What does that have to do with Nacho?" I asked.

Ms. Arabella paused. Then she said, "Camilla is allergic to rabbits. Our gym teacher, Mrs. Hanover, is going to take Nacho home to live with her."

We all wailed.

"No fair!"

"He was the best class pet in the whole entire school!"

"He'll be so sad without us!"

"When Camilla arrives," Ms. Arabella interrupted us in a loud voice, "I expect all of you to give her a warm welcome."

"We will, Ms. Arabella," said Jacob.

He is secretly in love with Ms. Arabella.

Which is ridiculous because *I'm* going to marry Jacob when we grow up. I've told him that a million times.

First no Nacho, and now we were supposed to be nice to the girl who made us get *rid* of Nacho? I stood up and banged my fist on my desk.

"A person who is allergic to rabbits has no business going to school!" I declared.

"Sit down *now*, Piper," said Ms. Arabella.

I sat back down in my chair and *hmmph*ed.

I guessed Jacob's father was right after all. Four lucky things *does* equal bad luck. And the bad luck's name was Camilla.

CHAPTER SIX

THE OPPOSITE
OF A BINKY

The first thing I did when I got home was to run to my bedroom. It was the lime greeniest thing I had ever seen in my life. The walls were lime green, the ceiling was lime green, my furniture was lime green. Mom had even painted my bed's headboard lime green.

I gasped. Because I suddenly realized something horrible. Lime green *is* the color of the Wicked Witch's face from *The Wizard of Oz*!

And then I realized something else even more horrible.

I was going to have to sleep in a room painted like a wicked witch face!

I went to the kitchen, where Mom was scrubbing a paint roller in the sink.

"Guess what?" I said. "I've decided that lime green might not be my favorite color after all."

Mom turned around and looked at me. Her eyebrows were lifted *waaay* up on her forehead. There were splatters of lime-green paint on her T-shirt and her jeans. There were even lime-green splatters in her hair.

"*Excuse* me?" she said in her scary voice.

"Nothing. I didn't say anything," I told her.

"That's what I thought," she answered. Then she went back to scrubbing the paint roller.

The door opened and Dad walked in. He took off the big black rubber boots that he wears on his lobster boat. Then he put his lunch cooler and his coffee thermos on the kitchen table. He kissed Mom on her lime-green head, then me, then Leo. He smelled kind of fishy, but I didn't really mind.

"How did it go today?" Mom asked.

"The weather was snotty," Dad said, shaking his head. "The boat was pitching like crazy."

"What was my catch?" Leo asked.

Dad always puts lobster traps into the water for me and Leo. When he comes home, he tells us what our traps caught. We get ten cents for every lobster.

"Let's see . . . Leo, you had five lobsters."

Dad reached into the change jar on the kitchen counter and dropped fifty cents in Leo's hand.

"Yes!" Leo said. "Twenty more lobsters and I'll be able to get a jumbo pack of Post-its!"

Leo is sort of a weirdo.

"What about me?" I asked Dad. "What did I catch?"

Dad curled his lips down into a frowny face. "Sorry, kiddo."

"Not even *one* lobster?" I said.

"Well, there was one—" Dad said.

I stuck out my hand for my ten cents.

"—but it was too small, so we threw it back," Dad finished. "That's the way it goes sometimes, pal."

"Tell it to the judge," I grumbled.

"Excuse me?" Dad said.

"I said, 'Peanut butter fudge,'" I told him.

Because my dad does not always have the best sense of humor.

I really needed some happy news, so I went outside to check if the Fairy Tree had left anything for me.

Coming up the road was Mrs. Penny-pocket and her bull terrier, Nigel.

"Afternoon, Piper," said Mrs. Penny-pocket. Nigel sat down right away and began biting at his tail. "I was just on my way to see your mother. I want her to have a look at Nigel. He's got a rash on his tail and it's driving him bananas."

Mom is a nurse, but since we don't have a vet on the island, everyone takes their animals to her too.

"What are *you* doing?" Mrs. Penny-pocket asked.

"I'm checking to see if the fairies left a treasure for me," I told her.

"Well, I guess Nigel and I will just wait and see too," said Mrs. Pennypocket.

I climbed up into the Fairy Tree. When I reached where the hole was, I stuck my hand inside and felt around.

My fingers touched something small and smooth.

"Hey, Mrs. Pennypocket!" I yelled out. "Guess what? There *is* something!"

"Go on! Let's have a look at it!" Mrs. Pennypocket said in an excited voice. Even Nigel seemed excited. He stopped biting at his tail and was staring up at me.

I scooped up the thing and took it out of the fairy hole.

"*Oooooh!*" I said. It was a beautiful dan-gly earring made of blue and green pieces of sea glass.

I held it out for Mrs. Pennypocket to see.

"Well, now that's wicked glamorous," said Mrs. Pennypocket.

"Plus, it's even a clip-on!" I clipped it on my ear and wiggled my head around. The little pieces of glass click-clacked against each other.

"Hold on," I said. "I'll get the other one so you can really see how they look on me."

I reached back in the fairy hole. My hand patted around in there. And then it patted deeper in the hole. And then it patted all over the place.

"There's nothing else in there," I said in a shocked voice.

"Maybe the other earring fell out," said Mrs. Pennypocket.

I climbed down the tree. Mrs. Pennypocket, Nigel, and I all looked around on the ground for another earring.

Nope.

"I've been having rotten luck all over the place," I grumbled.

"Well," said Mrs. Pennypocket, "my gran told me that the Fairy Tree always leaves you something that you really need . . . even if you don't know you need it."

"Yeah, well, no offense to your grand-ma," I said, "but maybe she didn't know what she was talking about, because what am I going to do with *one* earring?"

I slumped right down in the grass and put my head in my hands. I wondered what the opposite of a binky was. Because that's what I felt like doing right now.

CHAPTER SEVEN

WICKED WITCH ROOM

The next morning, I was totally exhausted. That's because I was awake for most of the night, being terrified of my wicked witch room.

Every time Mom or Dad popped their heads in, I was looking right back at them.

"Go to sleep already, Piper," Dad said.

"The problem," I told him, "is that Glunkey and Jibs are nervous because they've never slept in a lime-green room before. So how about tonight we all sleep in your room?"

He wasn't crazy about that idea.

Apparently, the Tooth Fairy was also afraid of my room, because in the morning, my tooth was still under my pillow and there was no *ka-ching*.

And worse . . . guess what today was?

Camilla day!

After breakfast, I clipped on my one dangly sea-glass earring, just in case Mrs. Pennypocket's grandma knew what she was talking about.

"Where did you get that earring from?" Mom asked.

"I found it in the yard," I said, which was sort of true.

"Okay. Well, remember, Piper, today is

Camilla's first day at school. It's scary to be the new kid, so do your best to be nice to her."

"Yuppers," I said.

I smiled at Mom.

She stared at me.

I saluted her.

"Why do I suddenly feel worried?" she asked.

When we got to the *Maddie Rose,* Camilla was already in the wheelhouse. She had long red hair. She didn't look scared at all. She was eating one of Mrs. Grindle's corn muffins and she was talking to all the kids. I grabbed a muffin real quick and went out on deck.

"So, listen," I said to Jacob, "when does all this bad luck go away? Because I'm about at the end of my rope."

He shrugged. "My dad never said. By the way, do you know that you're wearing only one earring?"

"So what?" I told him. "Pirates do it all the time."

Just then, who do you think walks right up to us? Camilla!

"Mr. Grindle said I might get seasick, since I've never been on a boat this small. He thought I might feel better if I stood out on the deck. I don't think I'll get seasick, though, because the weird thing about me is that I hardly ever vomit. Seriously, I think I've only vomited, like, twice in my whole life. I get hiccups all the time, though. Once, I hiccupped for five hours straight."

Boy, this kid sure was chatty.

"We moved into the lighthouse keeper's cottage," Camilla continued. "My dad is a carpenter, so they hired him to fix up the lighthouse. He's a really good carpenter, which does *not* mean he sells carpets, by the way. My bedroom is in the attic and it's really tiny. I used to have a *gi-NOR-mous* bedroom back in New Jersey. It was painted light blue."

Light blue! Suddenly that seemed like the best color to paint a room. Because there were so many nice things that were light blue. Like the ocean and robins' eggs and blue-raspberry ice pops.

If you thought about it, lime green was the *worst* color. Because the only things that were lime green were wicked witches and Saint Patrick's Day milk, which might just be leprechaun pee.

Right then I had another brainchild. I knew exactly how to bring Nacho back to our classroom!

"Hey, Camilla," I said, "I have something important to tell you."

I slid my eyeballs over to Jacob. He looked suspicious. I gave him a "mind your own beeswax" squint.

"What is it?" Camilla asked excitedly.

"It's about our teacher, Ms. Arabella," I told her.

I put my head close to Camilla's and said quietly, "Ms. Arabella is a witch."

Camilla wrinkled up her nose. "That's not true."

"She's a *wicked* witch," I said. "She has a giant tote bag, where she keeps all her witch stuff. It's full of evil potions and wart juice. If Ms. Arabella doesn't like you, she will put a spell on you and turn you into a hard-boiled egg and eat you for lunch. And guess what kind of kid she likes the worst? *Redheaded* kids!"

Camilla frowned when she heard that.

I felt a little bad about lying. But then I thought about Nacho. I bet he missed us. There were no kids in his new home to rub his head or give him toilet paper rolls to chew on. He probably didn't feel like doing binkies either.

"If I were you," I said, "I'd tell Mr. Grindle that you want to go *right* back home once when we get to Mink Island."

Then I remembered what Mom told me about being nice to Camilla on her first day. So I gave her a friendly pat on her back.

CHAPTER EIGHT

THE GIANT TOTE BAG

Everyone at school was excited to meet Camilla. They came running up to her on the playground before school started. They treated her like a movie star, just because she was new and because we only have fifty kids in our whole school. Ruby even gave her one of her lobster-band rings. It said "I heart soccer."

"How about hearting Nacho?" I muttered. "How about *that*?"

When we got to our classroom, Ms. Arabella had already written "WELCOME

TO OUR CLASS, CAMILLA!" on the blackboard in big, swirly letters. Then she sat Camilla in the special chair right by her desk.

"Good morning, everyone," said Ms. Arabella, smiling. "Let's all say hello to our new classmate, Camilla!"

Everyone screamed at the top of their lungs, "HELLO, CAMILLA!"

Except for me. I just made my mouth move. Garth belched it. His breath smelled like Cheerios.

"Sorry about that, Camilla," said Ms. Arabella. "We are an exceptionally noisy class."

"That's okay," said Camilla happily,

"because I have a cousin who never, ever, *ever* stops talking. She tells the same joke over and over again. What is brown and sticky? A STICK! Then she laughs and laughs. Then she tells it all over again. What is brown and—"

"I think you'll fit in just fine," Ms. Arabella interrupted Camilla. Then she turned to us and said, "Camilla's family moved here from the state of New Jersey. So, in honor of Camilla, we will be learning about interesting people who have lived in New Jersey."

Ms. Arabella put her giant tote bag on her desk.

Camilla gave it a funny look.

Ms. Arabella reached in her tote bag

and felt around. Then she lifted out a paper bag and put it on her desk. Out of the paper bag, she pulled a hard-boiled egg.

"Oops, wrong bag," said Ms. Arabella. "That's my lunch."

Camilla's eyes grew wide.

Ms. Arabella reached back in her tote bag and pulled out another paper bag. This one had a lightbulb in it. She held it up.

"Does anyone know who invented the lightbulb?" she asked us.

Hunter raised his hand. He always raises his hand even though he never knows the answer. He just guesses anything that comes into his head.

"Camilla's father?" he said.

"No, Hunter. It was Thomas Edison," said Ms. Arabella, "and he lived in New Jersey."

Ms. Arabella reached back into her tote bag. This time she pulled out a box covered in tinfoil. She put it on her head. It had a hole cut out of it so that you could see her face.

She looked around at us. "Who would wear a helmet like this?"

Hunter raised his hand. Ms. Arabella looked around the class to see if anyone else had their hand up. No one did, so she had to call on him again.

"Hunter?" said Ms. Arabella.

"My uncle Phil used to wear a helmet like that. But Mom says he's better now that he's on medication."

Ms. Arabella sighed. You could hear the sigh and everything. I think we exasperate her.

"It's an *astronaut's* helmet, class," she said, taking the box off her head.

"Ohhh!" we said.

"Astronaut Buzz Aldrin was the second person to walk on the moon," Ms. Arabella told us. "And guess where he was born?"

"New Jersey!" we all shouted happily, because we actually knew the answer to that question.

Ms. Arabella reached into her tote bag. This time she pulled out a magic wand.

Camilla's eyes got very big.

Ms. Arabella swished the wand around.

"What about this?" she said.

Swish, swish.

Camilla made a squeaky sound.

"Everyone knows what this is, right?" Ms. Arabella said.

Swish, swish.

"Who would use one of these things?" she asked.

"A WICKED WITCH!!!" shrieked Camilla. She jumped out of her chair and ran like crazy out the door.

CHAPTER NINE

BIG TROUBLE

After that incident, everybody wanted to hear My Own Words.

First it was Mrs. Waterman, the principal. She called me into her office and asked me what I had said to Camilla.

"Well, I guess you must already know, right?" I said. "Or I wouldn't be sitting here."

"That's true. But I want to hear it in your own words, Piper," Mrs. Waterman said.

So I told her.

Actually, it didn't sound like such a great brainchild when I said it out loud.

After that, Ms. Arabella wanted to hear the story in My Own Words too.

When I got to the wicked witch part, I thought her face would turn bright pink. But it didn't. It just looked sad.

"Do you really think I'm like a wicked witch?" she asked.

"No! I really don't, Ms. Arabella. I mean, sometimes you get a little crabby, but you do lots of nice things too. I only said that to Camilla because I want Nacho to come back."

"Hmm, I see." Ms. Arabella looked at me carefully. "Piper, you have a lot of passion. Do you know what that means?"

I thought about it for a moment.

"That I feel things with all my heart?" I said.

"Exactly. And that's wonderful. All those important people I was talking about today had a lot passion too."

"Even the witch from New Jersey?" I asked.

Ms. Arabella looked confused. Then she said, "Oh, you mean the person who uses the magic wand! That wasn't a witch. That was a magician. David Copperfield. And yes, he is passionate about magic. It's good to be passionate, Piper. But you also have to think things through before you speak. Camilla was very upset. She was so afraid to come back to our classroom that Mr. Grindle had to take her home early. He said she just sat in the wheelhouse and cried the whole time."

"Oh."

My eyeballs felt hot and wet. Ms. Arabella put her box of tissues in front of me. I took one out and wiped my eyes.

"But tomorrow she will be back in our classroom, Piper, and I want you to find a way to make her feel comfortable here."

I nodded and sniffled.

"By the way," said Ms. Arabella, "I went to visit Nacho last night. Mrs. Hanover said that our class could come to her house and visit him whenever we like. She owns three other rabbits, too, and Nacho has a new rabbit best friend named Cocoa."

"He does?" I said. My voice sounded croaky.

Ms. Arabella nodded. "He seemed very happy, Piper. He was doing that thing. . . ."

And then do you know what Ms. Arabella did? She stood right up and she did a binky. For real. She looked like a total madman.

The people who were the most interested in hearing My Own Words, though, were my parents. Mrs. Waterman had already called and told them what happened. Still, they kept saying, "*What* did you tell that little girl?" When I told them, they

said, "Wait . . . let me get this straight. You told her WHAT?"

Then I had to tell the whole story all over again.

"Well, I was planning on bringing my blueberry-molasses cake to Camilla's family after dinner," Mom said. "But I think we had all better go there right now so you can apologize. *Profusely.*"

"Does that mean the same thing as passionately?" I asked.

"Pretty much," Mom said.

CHAPTER
TEN

MERMAIDS

The lighthouse keeper's cottage is just a quick walk down the road from our house. It's a little white cottage that sits right next to the old lighthouse. There was a big yellow moving van in front of it. Dad knocked on the door. A tall lady with short red hair and freckles all over her face answered it.

Mom held out her blueberry-molasses cake to the lady. "Welcome to Peek-a-Boo Island," Mom said.

"Oh, thank you!" The woman took the cake with a nice smile.

"We're the Greens," Dad said. "We live just up the road a piece. The gray shingle house with the red trim. Stop by any time."

"I'm Leo." Leo held out his hand. Camilla's mom smiled and shook it.

"Pleased to meet you, Leo," she said. "I'm Mrs. Mackie."

Leo reached into his back pocket and pulled out a folded piece of paper. He unfolded it and held it up. "This is my wife, Michelle," Leo said.

"Nice to meet you, Michelle," Mrs. Mackie said to the paper. She didn't even give him the old hairy eyeball or anything. "And what's this here?" She pointed to a drawing of a dolphin on the corner of the paper.

Leo made a grimace. "Michelle got a tattoo the other day." He leaned close to Mrs. Mackie and said quietly, "I'm not happy about it, but what are you going to do?"

"And this"—Mom gave me a little nudge forward—"is Piper. I believe she and Camilla had a little misunderstanding at school today. Piper wants to apologize to her." Mom glared at me. *"Profusely."*

"Yes, we heard about what happened," said Mrs. Mackie. I waited for Mrs. Mackie to ask me to tell it in My Own Words. Instead, she said, "Camilla is playing down on the beach, Piper. Why don't you go join her?"

"O-kaaay," I said nervously. I didn't think Camilla was going to be too happy to see me.

I walked down the steep, scratchy path that led to the beach. Camilla was squatting by a tide pool, poking at seaweed with a stick.

"Hi, Camilla," I said.

She didn't say anything, which was definitely strange for a chatterbox like her.

"I just want to say that I am extremely sorry for telling you that Ms. Arabella is a wicked witch," I told her. "I am sorry with all my heart."

Camilla nodded.

"She's not really a wicked witch, you know," I said.

"I know," Camilla replied.

I squatted down next to her.

"I only told you that because I wanted Nacho to come back. He's our class rabbit, but we had to give him away because you're allergic. That's why I tried to scare you—so you wouldn't want to come to our school."

My Own Words sounded pretty mean actually.

"I didn't know about Nacho," Camilla said. Then she sighed. "I wish I wasn't allergic to rabbits, because I love them. I'm also allergic to cats, horses, and hamsters.

Plus guinea pigs and mice and goats. Also flowers and dust. If I'm even around that stuff, I start sneezing like crazy."

"Wow. That stinks," I said.

"I know it," Camilla agreed.

"Hey!" I said suddenly. "Are you allergic to periwinkles? Because there's one right next to you."

"Oh!" Camilla jumped to her feet and looked at the ground. "Isn't a periwinkle a flower?"

"This is a different kind of periwinkle." I picked the tiny little snail off of a rock and I held it out for her to see.

"Awww, what a cute little guy," she said.

"I don't think I'm allergic to periwinkles."

"Hey, I have an idea!" I said. "Let's look for other things you're *not* allergic to."

We found some blue mussels that she wasn't allergic to. We found an eensy-beensy tortoiseshell limpet that was sliding along a smooth stone. Camilla wasn't allergic to that either.

I picked up a rock and a little crab was underneath it. We didn't pick up that guy because crabs are so pinchy. But I found some nice, long pieces of seaweed. Camilla wasn't allergic to those either. I showed her how to be a mermaid by wrapping seaweed around your head. We looked very lovely. My mermaid name was Bibi Long-tail and Camilla's mermaid name was Lala Sparkles. We were each standing on a rock, posing our beautiful selves, when all of a sudden I heard clicking in my ear.

Click, clackety-click!

Camilla gasped. She was staring at me with a funny look on her face.

Click, clackety-click!

"Oh my goodness, Piper, don't move a muscle!" Camilla cried.

"What? WHAT? WHAT????" I said.

"Shhh!" Camilla pointed to my shoulder.

I kept my head very, very still, but out of the corner of my eyeballs, I could see

something green and yellow sitting on my shoulder.

"It's a parakeet," Camilla whispered, "and it's pecking at your earring."

CHAPTER
ELEVEN

GOOD LUCK

Very slowly and carefully, I walked back up to Camilla's house. The whole time that bird just sat on my shoulder and kept pecking away at my earring.

Click, clackety-click, click-click!

The earring swung back and forth. The sea glass tickled my neck, but I didn't laugh or anything. I just walked stiff, like a robot, so the parakeet wouldn't get scared.

When we got to Camilla's house, everyone was sitting on moving boxes in the living room and eating blueberry-molasses cake off of paper towels.

"No sudden moves, okay, guys?" Camilla said to them. "But look what's on Piper's shoulder."

Everyone looked.

"Oh my gosh!" cried Mrs. Mackie.

"Is that a parakeet?" my dad said.

They all walked up to me very quietly. Suddenly the parakeet stopped pecking. I worried that he might fly away. But I guess he just loved that earring too much, because after a few seconds, he started pecking again.

With her fingertips, Camilla reached out and stroked his feathers very gently.

"Well, he was obviously someone's pet, since he's so tame," said Mr. Mackie.

Dad frowned. "I can't think of anyone on Peek-a-Boo who owns a parakeet. Can you?" he asked Mom.

"Nope. I don't think this little fellow is from around here," Mom answered. "He might have come from a long way off. I've heard of parakeets escaping from their cages and flying hundreds of miles away from home. I'll call around, though, to make sure no one's missing him on the island."

"It's funny that he landed right on Piper," Mrs. Mackie said.

"Maybe Piper reminds him of his old owner," Leo said.

Click, clackety-click, click-click!

"Actually, I think it's the earring that attracted the bird," Mr. Mackie said. "It looks like those toys they hang in bird cages, doesn't it?"

"It does!" Mom said. "It's lucky you happened to be wearing that earring, Piper. If you hadn't, that bird might never have been found."

It was *lucky!* I thought.

Which meant that maybe I had finally gotten rid of my "too much good luck" bad luck.

CHAPTER
TWELVE

PARAKEET GREEN

When we got back home, Mom made a bunch of calls to see if anyone had lost a parakeet. No one had. But Mrs. Spratt, who owns the island grocery store, had an old birdcage in her attic, and Mr. Aronson had some birdseed in his cupboard. Pretty soon, we had that bird all settled in a cage. We even stuck in some branches for him to perch on.

We put him in my bedroom, on top of my dresser. Mom and I sat on my bed and watched as he ate his seeds and drank some water. He fluffed up his feathers and let them settle back down. After that, he nuzzled his beak into his wing in a very cozy way.

"He must be exhausted, poor little thing," Mom said.

I squinted at him. Then I opened my eyes wide. Then I squinted again.

"You know what's funny?" I said.

"What?"

"He blends right in with the walls," I said.

Mom looked at him. "Oh my gosh, you're right, Piper. His body is the exact same color. Lime green. In fact, they shouldn't even *call* that color lime green. They should call it parakeet green."

I loved that idea! Because a parakeet-green room wasn't at all scary.

Just then, I thought of something.

"You know what? Camilla didn't sneeze even once tonight," I said.

"No, I don't think she did," Mom said as she put a towel over the parakeet's cage. I snuggled with Glunkey and Jibs. Then I asked Mom to pull the cover over us, just like she covered the parakeet cage. She did, but she left a little blowhole for us so we wouldn't suffocate.

Suddenly I had a brainchild. And this

time it was an excellent one. Right after I thought of it, I fell asleep. And guess what? When I woke up in the morning, there was *ka-ching* under my pillow!

The next day in school, Ms. Arabella said she was going to change my seat. It was just in time, too, because Garth has been trying to burp the entire "Jingle Bells" song.

Ms. Arabella put Camilla and me together at the desk next to where Nacho used to be. Only now there was a birdcage in its place, and inside that birdcage was a parakeet-green parakeet. The parakeet was happily pecking at a dangly earring that was clipped to a loop on the top of the cage.

"Since Piper and Camilla are the ones who gave us our wonderful new class pet," said Ms. Arabella, "they should be the ones who sit next to him. We'll all take turns feeding him and giving him water and cleaning his cage. But first . . . we have to name him."

She told everyone in the class to write a name they liked on a piece of paper. Then we had to fold up the paper and put it in her giant tote bag.

I wrote down the name Chippy. Camilla wrote down Mr. McFeathers.

After Ms. Arabella collected all our names

in her tote bag, she jiggled the bag around so that the names would get all mixed up. Then she brought the bag to Camilla.

"Would you like to pick one of the names from my bag?" she asked.

Camilla looked at that tote bag kind of nervously, like she was afraid that she might pull out wart juice or something. But she was brave. She stuck her hand in the bag and pulled out one of the folded pieces of paper.

"Go on," said Ms. Arabella. "Open it up and let's see what we are going to name our new class pet."

Camilla unfolded the paper. She looked at what was written. Then she made a face.

"Yikes," she said.

"It's okay. Just read the name out loud, Camilla," Ms. Arabella told her.

"I just did. The name is Yikes."

So that's what we had to call him.

It's kind of a crummy name for a parakeet, but maybe I'll get used to it.

The first thing I did after school that day was visit the Fairy Tree. I snuggled in close to the tree trunk.

"Hey in there," I said quietly. "Thanks for the earring. I know I wasn't too crazy about it at first, but it turned out to be a good treasure. It really did come in handy. I guess you guys know what you're doing after all."

I gave the tree a "good job" pat.

Then I added, "Just so you know, though, an electric scooter would come in handy too."

A little wind blew up from out of nowhere and a leaf flitter-fluttered by my face. It tickled my ear and made me laugh. And then guess what? The weirdest thing happened. I heard someone laughing right along with me. It was the tiniest little pipsqueak of a laugh. You had to listen extra hard to even hear it. And a second later, it was gone with the breeze.

THE END